THE BRUSING EGO

- Rahul D.

CONTENTS

The Bruising Ego

Prologue

What do you think will happen in this novella?

If this was a non-fictional tale, it would seem apt to talk about Ego and how its existence can lead to misjudgment. At times, it can be averted but there are a few moments when it produces a ripple effect that chases us for a very long time.

The impact of this trait is so intoxicating that one deluges in its potency without even realizing. However, as much as one is captivated by its attachment, the disconnection can push them into the ravine. Thus, bruising someone's ego is effortless and elementary.

Ego doesn't always emerge on its own accord. At times, the circumstances and alternatively, premeditated instances allow it to place its cards on the table unhinged. The effect or its intensity remains in stealth mode till defacement shows efficacy. Either we are too deep to withdraw in that stance or we apostatize with the first exit, unless someone makes us comprehend our true nature. It cannot be just anybody, it must be someone special who has that influence on us. Perhaps, fate allows us to have that connection or maybe it just happens by chance? No one really knows but it does happen and there is some divinity in that bond. Let's figure it out as we initiate with our lead driving the opening act.

Everything that happens in here, will have a direct impact on the lead. This is a first-person narrative and would have relative reference to the directing personas, as they are introduced in this storyline.

1

I was strolling in the streets of a state within US, when I saw a street merchant with a big banner quoted 'Auction'. I got curious and asked what it was all about, as I had never seen an auction in the streets like that.

He said that he has a bunch of valuable items that he sells every day to the highest bidder, if I wish to enroll before the auction begins then I can but once I do, I won't be allowed to back out, as he will make me sign in a few documents which will make it official. Also, the big bonus was that there was no base price.

I thought to myself that since there are no competitors around, if I really find something valuable, I could probably get it at a nominal price, so I enrolled for it. The minute I did, two other individuals from opposite directions came along. One of them inquired in a similar way I did, and they signed in as well.

This was unlike any auction I have ever been to; I didn't understand how valuable were the items that were being auctioned, but from the look of it, it appeared to be old and priceless, which made me gain some interest.

The first item was put on display, it appeared to be a belonging of a famous deceased personality, they say if a person has died then the value of their belonging rises exponentially. The auctioneer asked for a base price. I said 10 dollars and immediately the guy on my left took out a brand new 100 dollar note and slammed it on the table, where auctioneer was sitting and said, "I see you and I raise you 10-fold".

I didn't realize how big that person was until he slammed that note on the table, he was over 6 feet 7 inches tall, almost like the Undertaker with an equivalent level of physique. He had tattoos all over his body. He looked like an old American bad boy kinda dude who is usually seen riding a Harley Davison bike.

I stood there staring at the way it all transpired, the other guy who was on my right took out 200 dollars and slammed it in a similar way. This was an aggressive auction; boy was I in the wrong part of the town to have encountered with the most influential beings I have ever seen. This other guy was as tall as I was, but he also appeared to have a good physique. If I had to bet on it then I would say more than just a 6 pack of abs, maybe 8. He also appeared to be richer i.e. it felt as if his aura was that of a rich guy, with branded attire.

They appeared to have a cat and dog rivalry, as they kept on slamming money on the table. At last, the richer guy won at a whopping 900 dollars.

The next item was the first edition of a comic book which I have heard could go for millions, if they were in a mint green condition which it was. The big guy started the price with another 100 bucks, the richer one gained control of the situation slamming 300 bucks and they both, along with the auctioneer looked at me, which made me embarrassed.

I am not a greedy guy but the way these guys looked at me, it seemed as if I was a miser, but believe me when I say this, this didn't look like an auction but more like a gambling table, where I was forced to be a part of so I can prove that I am also the big fish. I hate misers then how can I be one? My mind started playing tricks on me as my grey matter lost the battle.

I took out a 500 dollar note and was in the auction. To my surprise these guys got even more aggressive and started slamming even bigger bucks, so much so was the tension that the value just got raised over the bar, we were talking about thousands now. My last bid was 1500, after which I folded. You want to know where it got finalized? If you think 1500 bucks is huge then you haven't seen anything, this time the big guy entered the big game and slammed 11,500 dollars to get the comic book. I just wanted this auction to end. I was feeling miserable and really-really tiny in front of these people.

But I had to sit till the end of the auction as per the clause even if I don't buy anything.

This time, the item on table was a poster signed by a famous personality, they started the auction at 500 bucks, slammed by the rich guy, I raised the bar to twofold and became as aggressive as they were. I went on as high as 5000 bucks but, this rich guy was determined to take away the price to a whole new level, the other guy folded early. I was feeling proud that at least now I am not at the bottom of the chart.

When we were at 7000 bucks, a strange thing happened, this guy said "Oh, this is the picture of the hunter" and then folded as well. I won . . . finally I won but the way he folded, I felt suspicious.

Coincidentally, that was the last item in the auction and the auctioneer started to pack up and walk away, with the big bucks he collected today.

I looked at my signed vintage poster and felt like I was holding my fortune. But then a strange alliance was seen which shook my world. I felt this dreaded feeling which was unexplainable. All three of them, the two guys from the auction and the auctioneer were walking side by side. I just had to follow them. I realized that they were interacting as if they had known each other for years.

I joined in from behind to rejoice on our fortunes, they were least concerned as if I were the black sheep.

Now my suspicion grew stronger and I started making comments as if I know what's going on.

I said, "You guys are getting along well, you guys know each other? "

The tall one said, "I just had a good deal, does it hurt if we do get along well?".

I continued "Oh, you are going to the parking lot, is it just a coincidence that all three of you have parked your vehicle in the same parking lot when there are over a dozen lots in this vicinity?"

The richer one replied, "This one is the nearest, why would it matter? Where are you getting at?"

I continued "Another major coincidence, you guys have your cars parked in a sequence, next to one another."

This time the auctioneer replied, "What do you know, it is a day of pleasant coincidences and mixed fortunes."

My closing remarks to them made my suspicion into a dreaded reality, "You know that I am going to the cops after this, right?"

All three responded at the same time "We know."

That was it! I knew that I was conned and there wasn't anything I could do about it as it was a legit con!

All I could do at that moment was to watch them take my hard-earned money away in their respective vehicles. I felt like a nincompoop, but I wasn't perhaps their first one.

Things were popping in my head such as revenge, betrayal, 'I knew it all along and yet I fell for it', 'it is a disgrace to my intelligence', 'conned for the first time in my life', 'what will the cops think?'.

Maybe this is a dream? Let's do the old pinch thing:

Ouch!

I am awake, it was a dream!!

Perhaps a dream that I need to turn into a story one day, 'Conning the convict', wait that shouldn't be the title. This should be a secret, for now let's keep it the way it is, a dream!

2

It wasn't a dream, I simply spaced out for a while, I was still on the streets!

My mind was blank, perhaps for the first time in my life. It took me some time to regain my consciousness, but the moment when I did, I raced to the nearby police station and explained them as delicately as possible of the events that transpired right before me. They had this dull look as I narrated the whole thing.

Then finally the ice was broken with these verses –

"So, the only proof that you have of being conned is a hunch?"

"Well, I did cross-question them, to verify my intuition."

"You haven't even got the poster checked for authenticity before coming here and now you are playing the blaming game? This is not how it works son."

He had a point. I was so sure of being conned that I neglected all the other possibilities. I thanked him and contacted a buddy of mine who is good with strangers and has plenty of contacts up his sleeve.

He gave me an address of a collector whose sole purpose of living was to collect vintage posters and artifacts with historical importance. However, that guy's place was a three-hour journey from my current location. The worst part was that I had lost all my money in that little stunt and now was officially a broke!

To add more to the sheer bad luck, I was out of gas. My "fortune teller" was now an hour away and he was stuck in a meeting. It will take him forever to reach my spot if I do request him.

I was a newbie to this town and my habit of keeping liquid cash rather than a card for urgency was finally kicking me in the gut. I had no clue over my next course of action here. This moment reminded me of a movie I saw a few years ago, 'Around the world in 80 days' and I thought to myself, those guys travelled all across the globe in 80 days without spending even a dime and I seem to be freaked out on a three-hour journey? I think I can make it, it's time to make my own story!!

I looked around for any way I could use for transportation. However, my major concern was keeping my 'out of gas' car safe in a storage area nearby. I thought to myself, the safest place would have to be a parking lot, but they are going to charge me. I finally decided to think of the present rather than of the inevitable future.

I parked my car and started to walk towards my destination on foot. It's not that trying to catch a free ride as a hitchhiker didn't pop in my mind, but I despise so many things that I, at-times run out of options, hitchhiking being one of them.

While I was walking, I realized how impossible that task was, since I have been procrastinating to go for gym from the past year with one thing or the other. I was slowly going out of breath, with no stamina in my tank, I thought to myself, 'It has only been half an hour, I am sure I can do better than that?'

Then I heard my inner voice say 'No! you cannot', my body had finally indicated the threshold, it was time to retire, but where?

That was the real question!

I was losing my vision, everything seemed that blurry, it was clear that if I walk another step, I was going to faint.

The entire incident replayed in my head as if I was reliving the most dreadful moment of my life all over again, I didn't have a contemporary vision anymore.

Maybe, this was all a dream?

Let's do the old pinch thing!

Ouch!

It was a dream. I am awake! Before I knew it, I had a roof on top of my head and I was lying in a bed, was I daydreaming while walking about 'sleeping here' or is it the other way round?

A lot of 'ings' there, that couldn't be true?

What if it is?

Let's do the old pinch thing again, quick pinch and check, pinch and check.

Ouch!

This is real, I am in an apartment! I am saved or kidnapped? I thought!

Last I checked, I was walking towards my poster guy, if that was a dream, I sure as hell never had purple walls in my apartment. I decided to get up but got startled by a soft and yet high-pitched voice.

'You are lucky that I am a doctor! '

3

She looked more like an angel than a doctor to me, especially when I first saw her. She was wearing this white dress that could have easily been one of those Christian bridal outfits, the only thing missing was a halo, else I would have been convinced!

"You got dehydrated" she continued, "It's a good thing that I was walking behind you when this happened otherwise, who knows what might have happened. Luckily, you fainted in front of my house, else it would have been a challenge to help you out there."

I think I was going through one of those phases that we usually see in the movies. I could just hear her mumble but couldn't understand a thing, it was like every single one of my organs were appreciating her or perhaps it was the drowsy effect, it's hard to tell but those were one of those moments that I might cherish for a while.

I finally came to my senses and sat on the bed, indicating that my state has improved. "Who are you again?", I asked in astonishment. "I am Shirley, Dr. Shirley to you, Mr.? " she wondered. The way she rolled her eyes, I wished that we were in a film with a cameraman and all, so I could rewind this moment and see it repeatedly. Have I gone crazy? A minute ago, I was thinking about my loss in finance and now this angel rescued me and that is all I could think of.

'She is a really nice person who helped me when I was in a miserable state, I can't just hit on her?' I thought to myself. Then my brain took control over my heart and gave me a perfect reason to freak out. "Where? Where is my painting. I had it in my hand but now it's gone. Where is my painting? " I exclaimed.

"Calm down buddy, it's just a painting, you weighed like a zillion pounds, I couldn't have dragged you inside my apartment just like that, so I asked for help. No one was willing to but there was this guy, who volunteered and in return he wanted your old painting. I tried to bargain the deal with some money, but he just wanted that so . . . " she responded nervously.

I had a reason to be annoyed at her, but her voice was so sweet that instead she saw a sense of contentment on my face.

"Did I just sing 'Soft Kitty' for you?" she said in confused manner, apparently, she was all ready to be yelled at and didn't anticipate my psychotic reaction.

I did realize the terrible mistake she had committed but no matter how mad I tried to be, I just couldn't, my mind didn't even let me pretend. I ended up saying in a rather calm voice "Well, in that case we should get the painting back from that guy."

I could see it in her face that she was feeling guilty about the whole thing so just nodded as a response.

We left her apartment as I told her everything that ruined my day before I met her.

"7000 bucks for a painting? What were you thinking? I couldn't earn that much on a stretch, and I am a doctor, an intern actually . . ." she stopped midway as she saw my straight face over her remark.

I saw that the street was totally deserted as if a storm was about to come.

"What did he look like? " I queried in a very soft-spoken voice. I didn't even know, I had that in me, but she just made me realize a whole new set of vocal cords that were unused until now.

"He was a tall man probably a touch over 6, with broad shoulders, he was wearing a cowboy hat and had this unusually long mustache."

"Was he riding a horse as well?" I smirked while saying that.

She just smiled, I was probably flirting with her now in my own way, the unspoken language of sarcasm!

"Did you see where he went after he helped you with my weight?" I asked.

"No, but I do remember him saying that he has a lot to do today and by the time this day is done, he won't be a cobbler anymore." "Cobbler, great! that's a start, we have narrowed it down from millions to perhaps thousands in this neighborhood." I sighed.

"Hey, at least we have some lead now. Let's ask my handy guy, he knows everyone here." she said with a delightful smile.

I continued to stare at her smile until it got awkward and those teeth were no longer in sight.

"Your handy guy? " I finally asked.

"Yes! I have this electrician cum carpenter cum mechanic cum paperboy, in short all in one, the handy guy, he knows everyone in the neighborhood. He will know where to look."

That delightful smile was back again while she exclaimed. I think I was going crazy; I have never observed any emotional trait that minutely in my life! It was strange but at the same time, my happy hormones were dancing from within.

"Alright, let's go then." I said in a reluctant tone, so it doesn't get awkward again. All I ever wanted was to see her smile like that forever. I would love to be in a place where the time stands still with her showing all these cute, vented emotions.

My daydreams were back again as I followed her lead.

We finally found her handy guy who was at his usual spot. If I didn't know any better, I would have considered him to be a beggar. His clothes were torn from corners. He was wearing a t-shirt that wasn't probably cleaned for days. He was a rather short, clean-shaved man who appeared to have gone through a lot. There were scars all over his face that somehow showcased his victorious souvenirs from work. Shirley described the guy the same way she did earlier to me, and he immediately spotted our target.

"Yeah, I know him, that's David, he is a nut job, what do you need from him? " he asked in a rather judgmental way.

"We just need to ask him a few questions. Where can we find him?" she asked.

"He is the most predictable guy in this neighborhood, he will always be found near that dumpster after 7 in the evening" he smirked as he pointed out to a dumpster across the street.

"What about his current whereabouts? " she asked curiously.

"Who knows, the guy is a total waste. He earns to get high by 7, no matter how he does it, so his whereabouts remain unknown before that time. He could be anywhere." he confirmed.

"And you call him predictable! Thanks anyway." she said sarcastically.

I was a little disappointed, the more I wait, the more I will hate myself for what I did. It was like a one long nightmare, as if I was falling in a never-ending pit. Of course, a part of me was rather pleased by these series of misfortunes. Well, it was obvious, I would be able to spend more time with the one that makes me smile without a reason, and that is perhaps the best kind of happiness.

"Looks like we need to find something to kill another 4 hours, before we can proceed with our productive searching." she said in a euphoric way, or was my mind playing tricks on me again? Perhaps, she is just normal, but my wayward mind is making me think that way.

Nevertheless, my smile was bigger than ever this time, it was totally involuntary and there was no way I could have controlled it. I was getting conscious because it seemed as if she was taking the hint, but that didn't stop me from doing, what I did best in front of her.

"You are being weird now. Are you always this jolly during the time of distress?" she said with a tinge of confusion on her face.

I was back in control after that remark and I was rather proud of my acting skills, the way I handled the situation there forth i.e. from an irreparable state of judgment.

"Well, that's how this world is, always trying to figure out what is in a person's head, rather than realizing that humor can only cheer up a person from the outside. But who am I kidding, I am still the same guy who got conned even when I knew it from within, before it happened! How dumb could I be? " I said with a rather tensed look.

"Hey hey, don't blame yourself for what happened, money corrupts a person, no matter of what kind that person might be. I would have fallen into the same snare if I were you, so don't think about it so much. I shouldn't have ever commented on your methods, they were working rather well . . . you almost fooled me." she said hesitantly in the end.

"Fooled you? How? " I said while looking a little surprised.

"It's probably nothing, I had this friend who used to smile at me whenever we met at work. He was obsessed with me. He started to even follow me home after work. You can meet him if you want to, but you have to visit the nearest prison, your smile kind of reminded me of him." she said rather playfully while curling her hair near the right ear. You would have to be there to understand the magnitude of cuteness at that instant. But then I realized, what she said, and my defense mechanism did the rest.

"Woah, I didn't see that coming, it's a good thing that you realized the reason behind my smile, I don't want to share the cell with him." I smirked. However, in my mind I was rather nervous. I could have easily been that guy, although I wouldn't go as far as stalking her.

"Hahahah, that's right, so lucky! on a separate note, what do you suggest we do for the next four hours? " she inquired.

"I haven't been to this neighborhood, so why don't you give me a tour as my guide?" I fancied.

"That would have been a better idea if I were from upstate. This is a dull place to live in. Well, I am only here because it's cheap and I just started my practice. I was usually out of cash when I used to lead my life lavishly. It's about time that I start saving something, just in case."

"That's a good thought, just don't gamble all your savings on some painting which you don't even have a slightest idea about, and it could easily be a fabrication." I contemplated.

"Hey, don't be so hard on yourself, you never know, it might change your fortune, why would David be interested in it the first place, if it wasn't the real deal? After all, the guy has earned on others' misery, he must have been a pro by now."

"Yeah, but first we need to find him or else I am screwed. He is my last hope to get back my hard-earned money."

"Let's get you to a nice restaurant so you could forget all about this, with a delicious dessert." she assured with a flutter.

"Now, out of the blue, your neighborhood happens to have something nice, nearby? It's about time though. I am starving!" I winked.

"Yeah, my brain skipped a few signals after seeing your frown face, so was determined to make you forget all about it when I came up with that." she said so effortlessly as if it was on her mind, from a long time but couldn't find the window until now.

Everything that transpired thus far appeared to be a dream from one facet to the next. Such instances don't happen every day. So, I decided to cherish the present and be a part of this journey of life as a passenger rather than a pilot, at least while Shirley calls on the shots.

4

"Umm . . . this soup is delicious, what did they add in it? It seems like a culmination of every kind of soup I have ever had!" I sputtered.

"There's no one in the world who has ever denied the divinity within the food they offer. However, they are poorly advertised, which is why there was no need for a reservation." she amicably responded.

"You know quite a lot about a lot of things, are you sure that you are a doctor? You seem to be far too lucid to be one. Their personalities are rather complicated." I jibbed.

"Never judge a book by its cover" she conceited.

"I would say that I got exactly what the cover advertised." I said playfully.

"What was that now?" it was that question mark look again on her face again.

"Nothing, I think I have immersed myself so deeply to its taste that everything else around me just feels soupy, like literally!" I vindicated.

"Haha . . . good one! So, what brings you here?" she asked.

"Well, you might have heard of this in the past and you might feel the urge to laugh. Just try to restrain it till I am done with my side of the story." I apprised.

"It's a deal! Speak before I change my mind." she said in a frisky way.

"Well, like every other foreigner, one gets allured to this land with the hope of being an achiever. I have come from a destitute part of the society. My family had a lot of debt and were in such a pitiable state that they sealed the deal of my life to pay it off." I said with some apprehension.

"What do you mean by deal? Human Trafficking?" she sneered.

"No! God no! They got me engaged to person from an affluent stature." I blathered.

"Oh, so you are married?" she said with a frown face which somehow was inversely proportional to the diameter of my smile.

"Well, I wouldn't say that I was not intrigued by the offer, but all of that was overwhelming. I asked a friend . . . and he was willing to help me out." I said after a long pause.

"So, he helped you in what way?" she asked with a leery look.

"He had some sources who got me a visa to the States." I exclaimed.

"In return for?" she inquired.

"Do you really think that he helped me with an ulterior motive?" I wondered.

"Everyone is selfish, you won't really find any selfless individual in this realm at this age or time" she said with conviction.

"Well, that was awfully blunt but yes, you are right, he needed a favor in return." I said nervously.

"I knew it! So, what was it?" she asked with glistening eyes.

"Well, he wanted me to set him up with the girl, I was supposed to get hitched to." I evinced.

"That sounded so made up, but I believe you. It sounds like a scene from a movie though." she said in a snigger-ish manner.

"In the past 12 hours, my life has turned upside down, exactly like a movie! It's like God has automated all of its creation and I am the prototype of his new tool wherein every use-case is being implemented on me." I said in a deep state of trance.

"That was deep and dark, how do you manage to capture so much negativity in one sentence?" she said surprisingly.

"I ... ah ... I" I stuttered.

"If everything has turned upside down for you all this while, then my influence might be on the negative side of things as well?" she said in a rather blunt way.

"I didn't say that." I said nervously.

"Tell me, where do I fit in this chest of miseries?"

"I ... ah ... I" stuttering for the second time in my life.

The moment she saw me in that state, a huge burst of laughter was seen while I continued to turn red and pale.

"You should have seen your face. You are so cute!" she said playfully.

That's it, that was the word I was looking for. Suddenly, every anxiety in my existence obliterated, I felt like I was in a paradise. Every single hair on my body reverberated with excitement.

"Omg, how can an individual show signs of delectation and tormentation in the same scene?" she said with a surprise.

"I think that's your impact on me. To answer your question, your influence on me is that of a balance. Your aura has a cleansing effect on me. You were concerned for my negativity, but I am not, as I stand next to the personification of positivity!" I said hysterically. It seemed like my feelings/emotions found their way out as I saw her blush more and more at each verse.

"So now you are speechless?" I said with some confidence.

"Well, at least I was stuttering." I said with a wider smile.

"Oh, I haven't really heard anyone talk about me on such a high stature, so your kind words were a little overwhelming for me." she said after a long pause.

"That sounded so made up, but I believe you. It sounds like a scene from a movie wherein you are the lead." I said playfully.

"Don't get too cocky. Although, it is sort of fun to have an open-ended conversation with someone. Usually, I have closed-ended only." she said with a little smile on her face.

"Perhaps, you never came across someone whose fortune lies with a nut job." I said with a flirtatious smile.

"There's that look again. That's reverse psychology, isn't it? I put you in this state and I'll get you out of it. Till then our alliance stays intact." she said with an embarrassed smile.

"Well, if that's the way how it would go, then I want this to go forever." I murmured.

"Did you mumble something?" she inquired.

"No, this food is delicious." I murmured louder so she could understand it this time around.

We kept on engaging with personal discussions, during which she came to know that the money I lost was my entire life's saving. She felt bad and insisted on seeking out David prior to the scheduled time near the dumpster. I was pretty much full so agreed to tag along.

We kept on roaming in the streets, window shopping for him in stores and narrowest of lanes without any fruitful outcomes. Eventually, she sat down next to a painted wall as I observed her.

"I don't know what's wrong with this world. This is the second time; I have wrecked someone's life." she said with tears in her eyes.

"Don't dishearten yourself, we will find him. If I may ask, how is this your second time?"

"Well, long story short, I made someone pay dearly because he didn't agree with me." she sighed.

"And since we have time to kill, what's the longer version of that story?" I showed a quizzical expression while inquiring.

"That I am a horrible-horrible person . . . " she said, almost bursting in tears. For a moment, I felt like bawling too, but then I got back in control of myself, and I held her head on my shoulder to console her. She gracefully accepted my comfort and stayed there for a little while.

"I think I am okay now. Thanks, I really needed that." she finally said after withdrawing herself gently from my shoulder.

"It's alright to feel this way, we have all been there, but we should just stay in this state once and get it over with, after all it is the thing of the past and has no correlation with our present moment." I said in a mollified tone.

"Look at you all calm and positive, I was supposed to console you, when did this happen? It looks like we have exchanged our auras already!" she said in a frisky voice.

"Being negative is not a bad thing if it lasts for an instance or a moment but to flare up a blast from the past might be unhealthy in the long run." I said with a tranquil composure.

"I get it, I am not strong enough to handle it. Once I am, you will know." she said craftly.

"You don't need to, as the past doesn't have any hold on the present, and I want to know the present Shirley." I suddenly frenzied.

"Looks like a monk has possessed you! What was in that soup?" she facetiously remarked.

"A little bit of everything good, perhaps that's why we are swaggering our way despite of loose ends." I twaddled.

"You are something, aren't you? One moment it is something for you and then your personality takes a 360-degree turn and you become something else, so unpredictable, I honestly haven't met a guy like you before." she dazed while saying it.

"Well, is that a compliment or a . . . " I wondered while I tried to decipher her verses one syllable at a time.

"I am not quite sure myself, it's just that most people I have met in my adult life, have always been on one side of the cliff . . . but you? You seem to be like that cartoon . . . you know." she said in a doting moment.

"What cartoon? You think I look like a cartoon?" I suddenly garbled.

"No, that's not what I meant, you know that cartoon with the rabbit, what's his name? There's this cartoon in which he plays all baseball positions, first base, second base, all bases, one with the bunny . . . he is so cute, I can't believe I forgot the name." she began to prattle on and on, trying to figure out that name, it was endearing to see her try, it felt like someone is making me watch all those cute cat videos at once. I knew the answer, but I wanted her to continue those cutesy ticks repeatedly for as long as possible. Then she clacked differently "Help me, will you?" as she patted my shoulder playfully.

"Bugs Bunny, I love that show." I finally cowped.

"Yes . . . thank you, that would have eaten me alive! How could I forget that bunny!" she felt some solace in saying that.

"Yeah, it's euphoric to watch that one bunny, besmirch every other character in the show." I gabbled.

"Again, that's dark, I don't think that the events that transpired in the past 24 hours are the only ones that are bothering you." she contemplated.

"What kind of a doctor are you? Are you a psychiatrist?" I remarked satirically.

"Isn't that true?" she probed.

"I guess . . . it is." I scotched reluctantly.

"At least, you didn't stutter this time, you can tell me, it really helps to share." she said as if in a zone of tranquility. It was so soothing, that I profaned for capitulating unconditionally.

"Well, it wasn't only my money in there." I finally broke the silence.

"Say what!" she sounded dumbfounded. So, I started my tale before there were any more surprises.

"I told you that I was from a substandard lump of this realm. It wasn't feasible for me to have enough to invest if I put all my life savings together." I spoke impetuously.

"But you were helped by a wealthy friend, weren't you?" she inquired.

"Not exactly, he helped me out with the ticket, visa and with a sojourn but he wasn't as wealthy as you think, plus I wasn't really interested in marrying that woman. I cannot spend the rest of my life with a stranger without even knowing her beforehand." I kept on faltering in between.

"As much as I would love to discuss about the latter half of your prose, I am scared to know from where you got the money, so without further ado, please enlighten me!" she vented on a panicky note.

"Well, I got a loan." I responded.

"Please say that was from a friend or a bank!" she pleaded.

"None of those." I informed.

"I don't like the sound of that at all." again saying nervously.

"It was a fair deal, they quadrupled my money and even gave an appropriate validity, I got it checked from an authentic legal source, it's a new thing that's been happening here." I vindicated.

"If you say so, but you would have to return them at some point. What happens if you don't?" she pried.

"..."

"Well . . . your silence scares me a little." she uttered in an eerie way.

"What happens when you don't pay the bank? You are in debt, if it's a mortgage, then you lose your belonging at stake. And in an unconventional way, a personal loan usually adds repercussions, such as added interests, surcharge or even imprisonment. A clandestine affair gives us ample time for return. However, if this affair is infringed, the consequences are not regulated by the respective regime but rather by a pooled team of solitary investors." I elucidated.

"You are making no sense to me except it does seem like you have made a deal with a convict legally." she unadorned.

"That's not entirely true but the gravity of the situation has some affinity. They can do whatever they want to without any legal obligations." I deterred.

"You are in a mess which makes me think that we should get your painting at all costs now. I guess I have some savings through which we can subjugate David." she proclaimed.

"You need to understand that this is my doing and I am going to make things right, I do not want to lose any further in this ordeal. Let's work on our limited resources and see where we land. Gambling is not my thing, has never been, and I certainly won't start that now." I blazed.

"Wow, you do have some pride, but I can understand that at times, circumstances make an individual go through great lengths beyond their code of justice. I am with you in this, and we will get out of it together." she hugged me while vouching for it. It felt as if my existence was coalescing with hers. It was a warm sensation, that somehow made me more hopelessly infatuated apropos her than ever before. I hugged her back and we stayed in that state for quite a while. A feeling of demurring every other pleasure but this moment, pervaded in my whole body. This was it, humans have been running towards monetary growth their whole life, when the kingdom of heaven has always been amongst us. All it really needed was a moment. This was it, and I could have stayed like this forever. If only I was a statue who would remain unnerved and uneffaced for eternity.

Before we knew it, the clock struck 7 and we could hear the chimes from a distance that broke our stance. She just smiled and started to walk ahead where David would be seen tripping any minute now.

5

It's already seven past five and there has been no sign of the so called 'predictable' David. Every second would inflate our nervousness. Yes, she was as windy as I was, we were now a team and I know now that there was something between us before we had even met. It appeared to be inevitable the way we blended. I haven't ever in my life been, so candid with someone, as I have been with her, in such a short span of time. It somehow felt like an unresolved emission, weighing from lifetimes between us. Also, now I knew how to be in a state of delectation, even during trying times. Her face was getting paler, but mine had a dateless glace. She noticed it and suddenly spoke:

"It seems like you are having a sundae in your thoughts!"

"No, I am very tensed." I discerned and certified a taut look.

"Wow, you are really good at this, if I hadn't known you any better, I would have thought that all of this, was just a gag. But I know that you are not very good at maneuvering your emotions." she visualized as she spoke.

"What makes you think that?" I baffled.

"Well, as a doctor, I deal with patients from all walks of life, and have attained this persona of perceiving their nature, while examining their symptoms. You have no idea the kind of talent I get carved by every day. You are not the first one, and I know when I see one, that hasn't gotten a chance to bloom up in their arsenal." She said with an utmost zeal that even I got carried away. Although it wasn't all true, I didn't want to be responsible for a hiatus, so decided to play along.

"I guess you are right, I haven't been given an opportunity to touch the ceiling of a few emotional aspects. Perhaps, when I do them all at once with you, or with these circumstances around, I lag in their fervent rejoinder and thus, mix up every now and then." I rogued impulsively.

"It's alright, you are not the first that is demented by the sentimental baggage. I'll treat you as one of my patients, and you'll learn your way in framing it out." she showed compassion as she spoke.

I just nodded but enjoyed every bit of her reactive flavors. She was right about one thing, I had never experienced this before, sure I've had people in the past who have showed me compassion and love, but it somehow felt hollow. But this time, I felt fuller, I felt complete, every little chapter that she unfolded in front of me, made an enduring effect on my inner state. Perhaps, I did have an emotional baggage that I wasn't aware of, and this was my rehab.

Time just flew as I listened to her, showing compassion for me in different ways, I kept on feeling something or the other, as her emotions of various gradients continued to emerge. She was looking at the time and I was looking at her. Soon, it was seven past 30, she appeared to have lost all hope, and just stopped uttering any verses, or showing any reaction.

This change hauled me off her transfix. I saw the clock and it was almost 8. I asked her to retreat home as it was getting dark now. She didn't want to leave me, but I kept on insisting. Then suddenly we saw someone hobbling two and fro from afar. She immediately recognized him to be David. He would limp a few steps forward and then go around the circumference of an imaginary circle backwards, fleetingly for a quarter of a distance, and then limp forward again. It would almost seem like he could fall any minute, but the guy had some stability even in that state. Not once did he fall, one could play bets on his little stunts, he appeared to be that good. It would appear as if this was his daily routine, which it was.

"There's no painting in his hand" she remarked.

"I don't like the sight of that" I showed jitters in my voice.

"He's drunk as hell; do you think he would be in a state of saying anything?" she mushed as David got closer.

"It's worth a try, let's try to get out as much as we can. Clearly he must have traded it." I loathed. She looked at my face as I said it and felt the responsibility of fixing things.

After a few minutes, we saw David have a free fall near the dumpster, as the handy guy predicted.

"Hey . . . Hey David, it's me." she exhibited.

"Wha. . . me who?" David munted.

"David, we made a deal for an old painting to lift this guy to my apartment." as she nubed at me.

"I don't. . . re . . . call" David fatuously responded.

"He's drunk and wasted, he won't be of much use to us at the moment." I muttered to her.

"I am not drunk, I am perfectly healthy and sane." said David as he got up and almost fell, but then found his balance. He heard my muttering, 'Was I that loud? or does he have extrasensory perception towards hearing?', I thought.

"So, do you recall what happened today, when you helped this fine lady here with my body?" I incautiously spoke.

"Body? What body? I am not that type of guy, did you kill someone? I am not gonna help you with that!" he rose and started to have a shuffled walk, every now and then he would drop to his knees, but would then straighten up again, as if escaping from the devil with strapped legs.

"Why did you have to say body? I was very careful with my words the first time I said it. Especially when he is hammered." She said with some posthaste.

"I guess I wasn't thinking, although, you do know that the way he's running right now, we can match his pace with a saunter." I whimsically remarked.

It seemed like a hare-tortoise competition, as we strolled past him, while he saw us in agony.

"What in the devil's name is this? How are you so fast? We were miles apart a few moments ago, are you a magician or Satan's minion?" said David as he snapped.

"Calm down sir, you helped me lift this gentleman when he was unconscious, to my doorstep, on Round Acre street, at around 9:45 this morning?" she said in a self-possessed manner that even I got mesmerized in her charm.

"Oh yes, I remember you dear, I actually didn't see the face of the other gentleman I heaved, although his built was similar to your friend's. I can recall it now, you gave me the painting of the one called Hunter, he died a few years ago, but was a legend in his time." said the enchanted David.

"Yes, that's it, where's that painting now?" I barged in after harking back that name 'Hunter', which was articulated by one of the bidders back then.

David started screaming like a kid the moment I astounded him. Shirley intervened and spoke in a celestial seraphic voice, that produced a soothing sensation, not only to David but also to me. I realized that it was best to stay sluggish, while she is in-charge.

"It's alright David, we can understand how hard this must have been for you. We simply want to know the whereabouts of the painting, as it holds an aesthetic value to us." she said in a pacified hush.

"I sold it to Dunder for a brand-new bottle of Balfour 1503 Rosé" he battered out promptly.

"You what?" as I walked closer to him in a vexed exasperation.

"Shhh . . . let me handle this." she hushed me swiftly.

"That's a great deal David, so where is he now?" said Shirley.

"Yes, I know, it's one of a kind variety, he'll be found in his mansion, that's located in the South coast of Western California within Fair Oaks." said David with jubilation.

"Thank you, David, I'll let you mind your business now, enjoy your wine." acknowledged Shirley.

We left the spot so we could be isolated from David, apparently, he can hear everything we say, or murmur even when he is that juiced-up.

"Okay, I know it sounds like a challenge, but we can't stop now, we need to follow this trail and . . . " Shirley was interrupted by me, as I thanked her for all the help. She was a little shocked and didn't know why I was thanking her like that.

"No need to thank me, we just kept on pushing down that road, and were just lucky I guess to have gone this far." said the modest Shirley.

"Luck had no role to play here, you have been an inspiration all this while, and I dare say, I haven't seen anyone as brave as you, I gave you an opening to depart when it was getting dark, as a young lady like yourself, shouldn't be in the streets. But you, you didn't stir, till David was here, you stayed with me throughout. I think you were going to the clinic, when you found me unconscious outside your apartment, weren't you? You could have easily casted me away back then. Instead, you skipped your daily bread and butter, and helped me out without another thought. You are selfless, caring and brave. So, there was no fortune without those traits above. After all, fortune favors the brave. You are the silver-lining that has kept me going. For all that I say thank you!" I raved unhinged.

She didn't utter a word, just came closer and hugged, tighter than ever before. For the first time in my life, I felt content, I felt safe in someone's arms. It felt like a little world of my own wherein I can spend the rest of my life in peace and harmony.

6

I decided to call it a night as it has been a frantic one for us both, with the pursue and following trails. I escorted her back home, the clock had almost struck eleven by then, and there was drizzling. She was still very emotional from the speech I gave a few minutes ago, she had teary eyes and seemed to have cried a river from within.

"I know all of this can be overwhelming, but I am happy to have gone through such a misfortune. My life was pretty much dull before I met you." I said as I walked closer to her and held her hands in mine. She couldn't stop smiling when I did that.

"You are saying your life is dull? Spend a day in my clinic, and you'll know what dull feels like, the redundancy that I go through couldn't be delineated in words. For the first time in so many years, I felt the thrill called life, and the unpredictability that it holds. Your misfortunes . . . I wouldn't use that term . . . they were a series of unforeseeable events, and it gave me a motive to be animated again. I should be thanking you, although I know that circumstances could have been better in our pioneer contact, but I am glad it did." and got even closer while she said those verses. I could smell her hair as she looked up at me. I could feel her minty fresh breath on my face. It was all so soothing, I hope I wasn't making a mistake, as I have in the past, but somehow this doubt obliterated the moment I saw her smiling face.

It was happening and it felt right, ever since the first time I saw her, that moment appeared to have ignited a chemical reaction which was leading to this very moment, the beginning of something inevitably euphoric. It felt right, as we got closer, her lips got acquainted with mine. They were very soft, it almost felt like I owned them. They were that familiar to mine, but not the kiss particularly. The kiss felt like the first-time kind, I am not proud of it, but I have kissed plenty back in my day, but have never felt like this before. It struck like the first blush, even after we retracted and she went inside, I felt as if we were still doing it. The feeling was so serene;

the kingdom of this heavenly realm was added to my tastebuds.

I think this feeling stayed even after I was in the bed, the softness of her lips and her presence stayed with me, so much so that for the first time in my life, I skipped brushing my teeth.

Before I knew it, it was morning again. I got a call from Shirley and listening to her voice as the very first thing, it made me overjoyed. She was already in trouble for skipping yesterday without notifying and regretted to inform that she might not be there today due to that. I assured her that I will handle the dealing. She wished me good luck and I could hear a peck of a kiss through the phone as a good luck. I felt as if she was right in front and she stayed on the call till I got off that trance.

"You day-dream a lot, don't you?" she giggled.

"Only because you aren't here, else you would have seen me in action too and witnessed my day-dream moment." I said with a smirk. She simply tittered and then disconnected the call.

I felt a little sad upon her departure, but I got my game face back in no time and headed forward to meet this Dunder dude in California.

It was a two-hour ride; I was provided with some financial assistance from my significant other. Of course, she knew that I was very adamant and wouldn't agree to it right away, so we ended up calling it a loan, which I'll return with interest once I revert my misfortunate situation. These were all my terms, well to perhaps keep my pride unblemished.

She knew that I wouldn't really bargain on this, so she apprehended how to make me accept enough to last a few days, without any liquid cash. I did tell her that encashment could be done through my credit card, but the girl had a point. It's better to be in her debt than the bank. So, I made her my bank with those terms. I know it's funny if you think about it, it's all about whatever makes us content, right? That's the endpoint!

I took a cab to the place where I parked my car, got its tank full and headed out to meet this Dunder dude. I arrived in his neighborhood and figuring out where he lived wasn't the hard part, everyone knew him. After all, there weren't many mansions that were named 'The Dunder Den'. As I entered his premises, I was surprised to see that he wouldn't visit anyone on random, so I had to give an interview to his so-called assistant first.

"Sit down gentleman, my name is Fred, and I will decide if you get to meet Dunder Dunder." said Fred in a rather rugged tone. When I first saw him, I thought that he's one of those bouncers that are seen outside a club (a bodyguard or security in this case). I even raised my hands as a sign of surrender when I saw him approaching me after entering the building. To my surprise, he was rather gentle, but his tone was that of a bouncer.

"Excuse me, Dunder Dunder? Why are we repeating his name?" I asked astoundingly.

"You are a complete stranger, aren't you? You don't even know that she's a woman." he said in a straightforward manner.

"I guess I never thought a woman to have the name Dunder, furthermore her parents were so obsessed with their family name that they would even first name her that. I mean that's child abuse. She might have had a harsh childhood."

My habit of scornfully cooking up things was kicking me in the gut today, especially when it was this important. Oh man, how badly was I missing the intellectual side of my significant other today. She would have handled this situation rather well. To my surprise, I didn't see any reaction from him.

"And you aren't even aware that she is married. She became Dunder Dunder after her marriage, sir." he said in the same monotonous way.

"I see, well I have a little business to tackle with Mrs. Dunder Dunder." I stirred.

"She is divorced but she has still kept the name as it has led to good fortune for her. We call her DoubleD, if you know what I mean." he said with a little smirk. This surprised me because I never thought that he was capable of any other emotion. It felt like talking to an autonomous robot until then. This almost spooked me.

"I see, can I meet Miss DoubleD if it's alright, I have a business proposition for her." I said patently.

"All her propositions go through me, if you think that I wouldn't be able to decode your jargons then, you may log all you want to say on a piece of paper. But I would suggest going for a presentation instead, as she is rather impressed with my dispensing skills." There was that smirk again while he delivered me that message. It spooked me every time, I think that I was starting to believe that first impression ideology now. I cannot picture him smirk like that, no matter how hard I try.

"I don't have anything to present, she has my hunter painting and I want it back." I pattered like a monkey. I think Shirley was right about me having trouble to maneuver my emotions. I just didn't realize it. What else is she good at? I thought. In that trance, I didn't realize that I almost freaked Fred who rushed back into the house while I stayed in that daydream. Geez, what else can go wrong? Suddenly, I could see Shirley right next to me. We are so close that we could feel each other's breath. I was surprised to see her, but then she got closer and then we kissed. It was all so real. I was embracing her with all my might as I kissed her hard. I forgot where I was and how fairytale like it all seemed.

I was caught in the moment, as we kissed passionately. I had my hands all over her hair, as we kept on swaying from side to side.

This kept on happening, until I was splashed with a bucket of water. When I opened my eyes after the splash, there are no Shirley. I saw a weird lady in front of me. She appeared to be dressed as a dapper, with a bob cut. If I hadn't known any better, I would have called it a wedding dress, but there was a lot of tweaking, which made it look like the kind that have been worn a lot. It appeared to be special and yet, the way it was altered made it look like a ballerina. She was a misfit, but she appeared to be proud of that attire, I could see a haughty look on her face. She had a strap in her hand which appeared to be shredded from places.

I suddenly realized that I was a captive, there were two huge men who had strapped my hands on either side, as if I was their present to the lady of the house.

"What's going on? Free me now, I didn't do anything wrong." I yelled.

"Release him, we were only limiting your movement, you seem to be pouting your face when we found you in the garden. Perhaps, you were having a vision? I do admire soothsayers." she simulated.

This gave me an idea and I am rather proud of this sudden nimbly plot.

"Of course, I was, in fact it's the vision that led me here, Fred would tell you that I am not aware of your existence, but these visions led me here. I am looking for something." I resounded so highly that even I started to believe my verses.

"Impeccable, what is it that thou seek, oh great one? Fred tells me that you seek for a painting, a very special one I might add." she appeared to be imitating someone, I had a hunch, and I went for it.

"I can sense that you have great love for literature, if truth be told, you admire none other than the great Bard of Avon, Sir William Shakespeare." I reverberated.

"Impeccable, you know your stuff so well, yes I exorbitantly emulate him, in fact I married my husband because he had traits of Sir William Shakespeare." she said in an excited voice.

"Yes, I see that to be true, but I sense that you have been divorced, why would you divorce him?" I said while looking at Fred who told me about it. And I was glad to see that his face was expressionless as always. I would hate to see him smirk at that.

"Yes, but I was referring to my first husband, the great Hunter Dunder." she said with utmost delight.

I suddenly realized that my painting was that of her husband! I was so in the character that I didn't exhibit my shock to her. I kept on playing it quite impressively, if only Shirley was here. That's all I could think of.

"Aah, I can sense that you have been collecting paintings of him, paintings to fill your void. He died a few years ago. And after your divorce, that void has recrudesced, and it is deeper than ever before. I can sense that you bought one recently, one of a kind portray." I pulsated the whole room with my voice, I didn't notice how empty her mansion was until then. There was no real furniture, just antiques of all kinds. And yes, then there were paintings, I still couldn't find mine though, I tried to sneak peek every now and then when I got the chance.

"Impeccable, so precise is your vision. That is correct, he was the love of my life, all this wealth is his, we fell in love and were happy until he died. He named his everything as mine in his will. Despite of all this wealth, I felt empty, thus Sergio came along, not even my servants are aware that Dunder was and has always been with me before Sergio, Sergio was younger to me, we were happy, so I thought. Until I realized that it was wealth he was after. So yes, it ended as it begun. But bravo to your vision. You are right, I did acquire that masterpiece recently." guised DoubleD.

This was my moment, I had to make it perfect, I had pictured this in absolute detail in my mind while she was dabbled in her husband's long-lasting memories.

I clutched my forehead and started to rub the two sides in a circle.

"I can see more, oh it is strong, I perceive that this painting that you acquired yesterday wasn't valued, he's very angry, you got it for such a meagre bargain that your husband has risen from the dead to show his retaliation, his spirit is vexed at you, you got his most prized possession by trading it, with a brand-new bottle of Balfour 1503 Rosé? He feels unappreciated, he is angry, I can't contain him much longer. My aura has pacified him. But I can't keep it that way for long" I said in utter anguishment.

"Oh God, I didn't know that this would happen, I am a business-woman and I found it to be a good deal. How do I fix it? Isn't there anything I could do to please him?" she asked clemently.

That's it, I was in control, all she needed was a final push, this was almost over. "He wants you to appreciate the painting, you need to acquire it the way it is felt appreciated. Bring forth the painting now and place it on this table." I squalled while saying it, as if showing vision spin-offs.

She asks one of her attendees to bring the painting, there she was, how long have I waited to see her, now I just needed to grab it and get the hell out before Fred starts flapping.

"You need to re-buy it but with a price that this painting is worthy of, only then will your husband be at peace again." I mustered.

"Yes sir, but I don't know where David is and frankly if I pay him, he'll probably swill himself up and might probably die." she said anxiously.

"No, you need to show this gesture, so your husband acknowledges it. And it shouldn't be anyone that lives in this mansion, it should be an outsider." I said hoping she would be able to decipher my gesticulation.

"What about you sir? You can take it?" she spilt what I wanted her to. I had played the stage perfectly, it felt too good to be true honestly.

"No, no, it doesn't work that way. You will have to re-buy, giving me money for the painting wouldn't seem right, I don't give service to my visionary gift. I cannot accept that at the same time." I caved as I was deluded in a battle to decide what I wanted.

"There must be a way, you said that you can't hold him any longer, how do we make him content again without this bargain?" she perturbed.

"It appears that there is a way, you need to displace the painting, it shouldn't be in the house." I slicked. I fancied that painting, but I know she won't let it go that easily, I can't play this game forever, it must end now.

"He won't allow me, he had desire for this painting even when he was alive, now that I have it, I can't let it go, money is garbage to me but that painting, it's priceless, there must be a better way, what does your vision say about that?" she almost inflamed.

I was getting weak in my strategy, so had to play around a little, showing her that I was getting a vision, but I was clueless, how do I get this painting? Should I just take the money but the worth of this art is still a mystery. I had an option here, either I take what I lost, or I figure out a way to get my painting back and ask someone for its real price. Perhaps, there's a third way.

"I didn't want to suggest this, but this spirit needs to be contained, I can keep it in its priceless possession for a day and then you can pay what this piece is worth and keep the spirit and your wall happy." I said these verses and immediately called it cliché in my head. They are going to figure it out that I am here for the painting and they seem to be very powerful people, I might lose more than just my money this time around.

"Yes, I think that can be done, but you should know that we need this painting, so make sure to return when it's time to." she threatened, it almost felt like a warning. I knew what I was getting myself into. So, I just nodded.

I did a little silent ritual, gestured to have caught the spirit and allowed it to plunge into the painting. I further asked them to cover it with a laminated sheet, to contain it. Then took it back with me, while they stayed there within the mansion unmoved.

I was shocked and sort of proud of pulling it off. I had my 'Hunter', the sky was bright again and I had Shirley in my life. I decided to surprise her upon her return.

7

"Hey you, I am sorry for not being there. And since, you didn't call all day, I know it didn't go well. But that's alright, we'll get this through, I have some savings that you can loan from me and return that money borrowed under your 'clandestine affair'. I have thought this through so don't argue with me, okay? Furthermore, we can always work together in getting you something which can help you in setting-up an establishment from scratch. I have had alliances with network of entrepreneurs over the years. It's time, we put that to use . . . .mm . . . ." she kept on pattering as I got closer and closer to her.

Yes, I kissed her to shut her up and she also got caught in that moment. She wouldn't stop, I made her think about our future all day, that's how much she cared about me, or I would rather say 'us' because, when two people feel deep affection for one another, they are not an individual entity, they unite, they integrate as one.

I guess, we can use a similar analogy on God. When an individual has perceived his/her God–Consciousness i.e. realizing his own nature of existence, all the veils that surround consciousness are obliterated. The thing or I should rather say no–thing is left, this is not a separate entity in itself but rather a raw rugged awareness that is now ready to unite with the universal consciousness. Once, the union is panned out. There is no 'I' in that form, but the culmination of all forms. Everything is a singularity.

This is how the state is when one has united with his/her significant other. There is no 'I' any longer. It always starts and ends with 'us'. Every instance of one's life leads to a decision, that undertakes each other's combined benefit, or I should rather say, every activity affects us rather than only one of us. As single entities are now just spectral.

"Wow, I think you wanted me to stop worrying and somehow this kiss did the trick for us both, way the go!" she said radiantly.

"I can get used to that radiant face. And yeah, I wanted you to stop worrying because I have something for you." I leered.

I took out the painting from under the bed and she got spooked. Unlike my past relationships wherein such a stunt usually means a breakup for the rest of the day, she acknowledged my gesture, despite of what she went through, because of me throughout the day, she knew I had righteous intentions. So, instead of reproaching, I was awarded with another kiss. And this one was much more passionate.

But she sure wanted to know my side of the story, I proudly presented it with particulars and dialects, as if doing a play. It was hysterical, fabled and heroic if you ask me. For some reason, she wasn't really impressed by all that, it baffled me.

"You know what happened here in case you didn't notice?" it appeared as if she was an arbiter.

"Well, isn't it impressive the way I nailed it?" I staggered.

"The thought is impressive but rather than thinking about execution, perhaps you should perceive what all transpired from another angle." again it felt as if she was scrutinizing.

"So rather than thinking what I did, you want me to think how it happened? Rather than the execution, I should understand the intent behind it?" I probed.

"Precisely, just think for a second, how your pursuit started and how it is ending? Who conned whom? Contemplate it!" She jolted.

I thought over it, she was right. I looked back to what I bumped into back then. I thought the auctioneer conned me because of the way that instance transpired. But the painting turned out to be the real deal, plus everything was legit. How can I call that a con?

However, what ensued based on events from yesterday was a con. I made DoubleD believe that I was legit and conned my way in getting that painting. Although, it was rightfully mine, it doesn't rule out the fact that I defrauded my way in attaining my want.

"I understand it now, unintentionally and with hubristic instincts, I became the one I despised the most. But what now? Do you want me to come clean? I think the only one who might be in a fuss would be me in the end." I said in a perturbed manner.

"I am not asking you to come clean here. You know why people are transgressors? They commit the crime without realizing. And the realization is grasped when empathy starts to play that role in their lives. The moment they do, the veils of being a hooligan are annihilated. So, the moment you realized the committed blunder, your debt was paid. However, that doesn't give us a free pass to play around. Know this that it is an exception because DoubleD is a wealthy woman, she is in love with Hunter, she believes that her husband is still with her and that painting holds great value in her heart." she declaimed.

"Your ploy would do her good, she will not only believe that her husband is at peace, but this will also fill her void which was getting cavernously close to infinity day-after-day. Let her name the price for the painting and you will graciously accept her offer. I do not want you to force her to raise the bar, just because she is rich. Let's not take advantage, we were already in a pitiable state. Whatever she has to offer, let's just accept that and be slightly less in our debt. Now that we are together, we will fight this through and lead our lives with honesty from here on." She bombastically concluded.

Could I love someone more than I already did? We kissed and this moment of passion was so extreme that the experience of being with her had a whole new equal. It was such an eye-opener!

She isn't only my soulmate but my guiding angel. I was on the wrong path and yes that was inadvertent, but I would have ripped off DoubleD if I hadn't realized it. Although, I was planning on mustering some intel from my sources, to know the price rather than giving her a ballpark number, but it was not a plausible thing to do. Shirley helped me in averting the most unjustifiable act I could have ever committed.

In the end, it is all about our ego, isn't it? Even when someone doesn't strive to, just the thought itself can bruise it. It is such an easy task to discern that change. People outstretch to new heights to preserve this ego. When in verity, it is our perception that makes us feel that way.

Ego is but a three-letter word. The moment you realize that, you break it!

Epilogue

Ego has ruined lives in unsettling ways. Most of them could be circumvented by breaking this entity in us. And yet, we don't. There's something idiosyncratic about this trait, it adds significance in our prosaic lives.

We just have to be right, don't we? Especially, if we are the captain of the ship. Then it intensifies exponentially with experience. Let's say you are quite young in your practice and manage to scrutinize a research paper by a learned scholar. Upon critically analyzing, you observe a few chinks that can disprove their observation. No matter how accurate your findings might be, the learned scholar who owned the paper would always try to find an escape clause rather than appreciate or observe your perception.

People always prefer credence over flair. Because the latter doesn't have a portfolio to showcase and might have humility due to limited exposure. However, the former would be blown with pride and ego due to their achievements over time. They don't say for no reason that accolades and fame could easily corrupt a person. It happens to the best of us.

Ego ensures that they continue to justify their approach rather than accept the flaw and grow with each blow to their proficiency.

What do you think went wrong here in our narrative? There was a chain reaction to the thought of the narrator, this was ignited by a single blow to his principles. The thought of being a miser when he despises their existence. The single thought started a chain reaction that was too strong to be contained within the realm of his thoughts. Eventually it surfaced and made him commit the blunder of a lifetime.

If you think that he was too sensitive to have fallen into that trap. Let me share a real-life instance - we traverse through millions of court cases every day throughout the globe. Each of those starts with the prosecutor accusing the defendant. No matter who might have an upper hand in terms of stack of facts. It's always the most diplomatic one that lasts the longest. Facts are manipulated and falsified, or near-truths are used as weapons against the accused. These circumstances can be overwhelming to anyone who might not have been exposed to this before. The lawyers know precisely which buttons to press to weaken the core of the accused. They get pushed with each bruised ego to fortify the opposite-parties' exposition. It might as well be a cock and bull story, but they narrate with such conviction and manipulation, that the jury eventually favor the dubious one.

We all need someone like Shirley in our lives to snap out of it or else, some convict might eventually learn to hammer our persona that bruises your ego to an extent of spanning another journey.

www.ingramcontent.com/pod-product-compliance
Lightning Source LLC
Chambersburg PA
CBHW060447160726
47992CB00003B/1110